Domenico Cimarosa
Three Sonatas

*Arranged for solo guitar by
Julian Bream*

First published in 1968 by Faber Music Ltd
Bloomsbury House
74–77 Great Russell Street
London WC1B 3DA
Cover design by Shirley Tucker
Photograph by Sandra Lousada
Printed in England by Caligraving Ltd
All rights reserved
ISBN10: 0-571-50198-2
EAN13: 978-0-571-50198-4

To buy Faber Music publications or to find out about the full range of titles available
please contact your local music retailer or Faber Music sales enquiries:

Faber Music Limited, Burnt Mill, Elizabeth Way, Harlow, CM20 2HX England
Tel: +44 (0)1279 82 89 82   Fax: +44 (0)1279 82 89 83
sales@fabermusic.com   fabermusicstore.com

Domenico Cimarosa (1749-1801) was a prolific composer. Apart from the many operas and oratorios that flowed freely from his pen, there are also a number of instrumental pieces, the most important of which are 32 harpsichord sonatas. While they may not have the extraordinary harmonic freedom of the sonatas by his compatriot, Domenico Scarlatti, they nevertheless reveal a most expressive melodic gift, characteristic of the Neapolitan style. This is particularly evident both in the first of the sonatas I have transcribed and in the third, the celebrated and sublimely beautiful Larghetto. The second, on the other hand, shows the sharp wit and good humour that has made his opera, *Il Matrimonio Segreto*, a perennially popular work.

Domenico Cimarosa (1749-1801) war ein äusserst produktiver Komponist. Neben den zahlreichen Opern und Oratorien von seiner rutinierten Feder gibt es noch eine Reihe von Instrumentalstücken, unter denen die 32 Cembalosonaten die bedeutendsten sind. Wenn ihnen auch vielleicht die ausserordentliche harmonische Kuhnheit der Sonaten seines Landsmanns Domenico Scarlatti fehlt, so entfalten sie doch eine äusserst ausdrucksvolle Melodik, wie sie fur den neapolitanischen Stil charakteristisch ist. Dies kommt besonders in der ersten der von mir übertragenen Sonaten zum Ausdruck sowie in dem berühmten Larghetto der dritten, einem Satz voll erlesener Schönheit. Die zweite Sonate andrerseits zeigt den Witz und Humor, die seiner Oper *Il Matrimonio Segreto* ihre Popularität über die Jahrhunderte erhalten haben.

Domenico Cimarosa (1749-1801) était un compositeur extrêmement fécond. En dehors de nombreux opéras et oratorios composés avec grande facilité, il existe une série de pièces instrumentales, dont 32 sonates pour clavecin sont les plus importantes. Si toutefois elles n'ont pas l'extraordinaire liberté harmonique des sonates de son compatriote Domenico Scarlatti, elles révèlent cependant un don expressif et mélodique caractéristique du style napolitain. Ceci est particulièrement évident dans la première des sonates que j'ai transcrites, ainsi que dans le célèbre et sublime Larghetto de la troisième. La deuxième parcontre se caractérise par l'esprit mordant et la bonne humeur qui fit de son opéra *Il Matrimonio Segreto* une oeuvre populaire et durable.

Julian Bream

Explanation of the following signs may be useful:
Die Erklärung der folgenden Zeichen mag für den Spieler von Nutzen sein:
L'explication des signes suivants pourra être utile:

·····	LH legato or slur. M.G. legato ou liaison.	Linke Hand: legato oder Bindebogen.
2·····2	LH finger indicated should remain on the string. Pressure should be released for a shift to another fret. M.G. le doigt indiqué doit rester sur la corde. La pression doit cesser au changement de case.	Die angedeuteten linken Finger sollen auf der Saite bleiben. Bei Bundwechsel soll der Druck aufhören.
⌐	LH fingers must be positioned before the ensuing phrase is played. Les doigts de la M.G. doivent être en position avant de jouer la phrase suivante.	Bevor die nächste Phrase gespielt wird, muss die Fingerstellung der linken Hand eingenommen werden.
CIII	Grand *barré*. Grand *barré*.	Grosser Quergriff *(barré)*.
III	*Barré* stopping 3 strings or less. *Barré* étouffant 3 cordes au moins.	Quergriff über 3 oder weniger Saiten.
⌐¹	Momentary *barré*, stopping the strings indicated by the bracket. *Barré* momentané, étouffant les cordes indiquées entre parenthèses.	Kurzer Quergriff über die durch die Klammer bezeichneten Saiten.
⌐	Natural harmonics are shown by a diamond note-head at their true pitch, with fret and string numbers indicated. For artificial harmonics, the diamond note-head shows the note to be stopped, while the forefinger of the RH touches the string above the fret indicated. Les harmoniques naturelles sont indiquées dans leur hauteur exacte par une tête de note carrée. Pour les harmoniques artificielles, la tête de note carée indique la note a arrêter, tandis que l'index droit se poser sur la corde au-dessus de la case indiquee.	Natürliche Flageolettöne werden mit viereckigen Notenköpfen in der richtigen Tonhöhe angezeigt, mit vorgeschriebenem Bund und Saitennummern. Für künstliche Flageolettöne zeigt der viereckige Notenkopf den zu stoppenden Ton, während der rechte Vorderfinger die Saite über dem bezeichneten Bund berührt.
[*p*	Notes indicated by the bracket to be plucked simultaneously by the RH thumb. Les notes pourvues de parenthèses sont à pincer simultanément avec le pouce droit.	Noten, die mit Klammern versehen sind, sollen gleichzeitig mit dem rechten Daumen gespielt werden.

SONATAS

Transcribed by Julian Bream

DOMENICO CIMAROSA
(1749–1801)

I

© 1968 by Faber Music Ltd.

F 0198

II

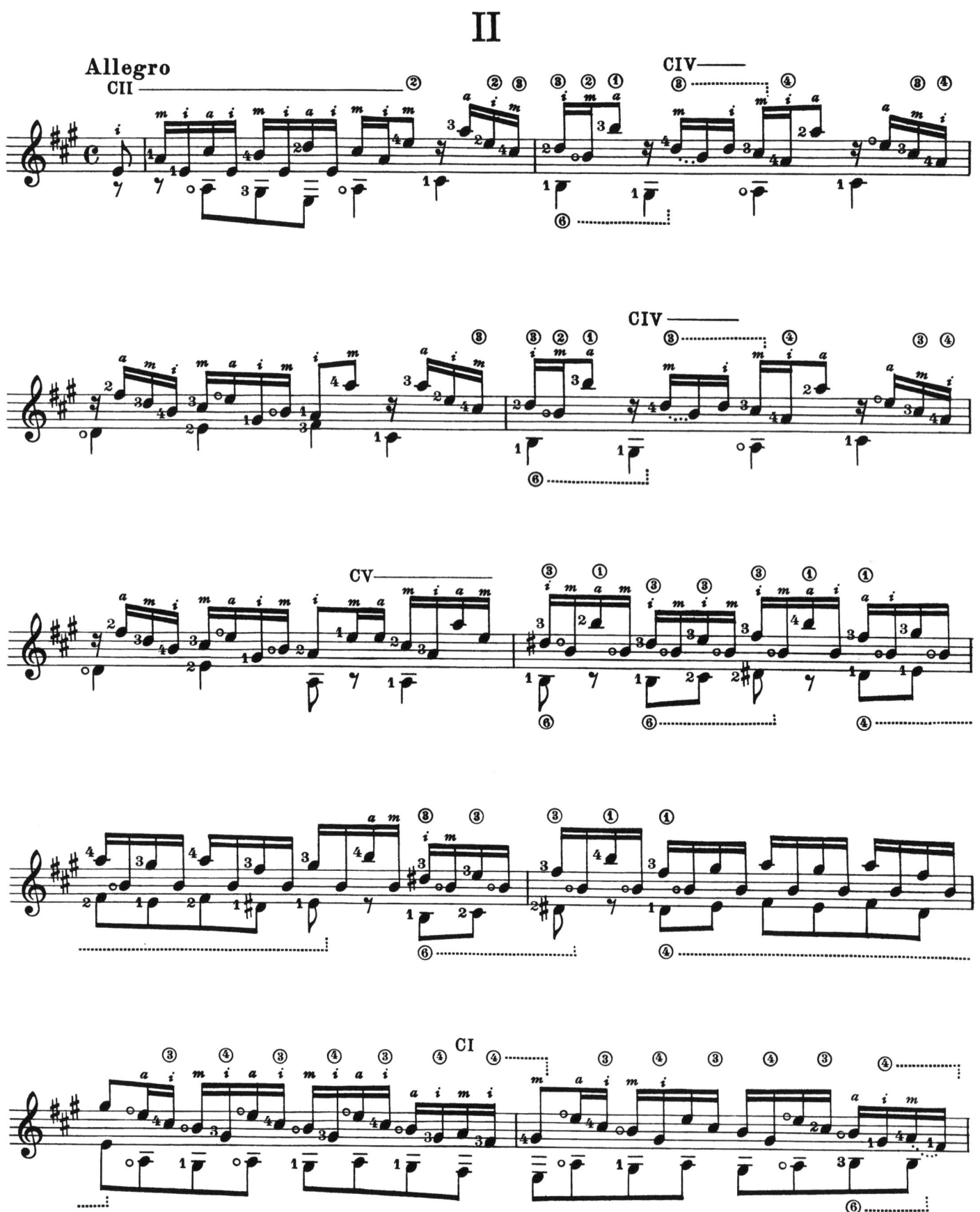

III

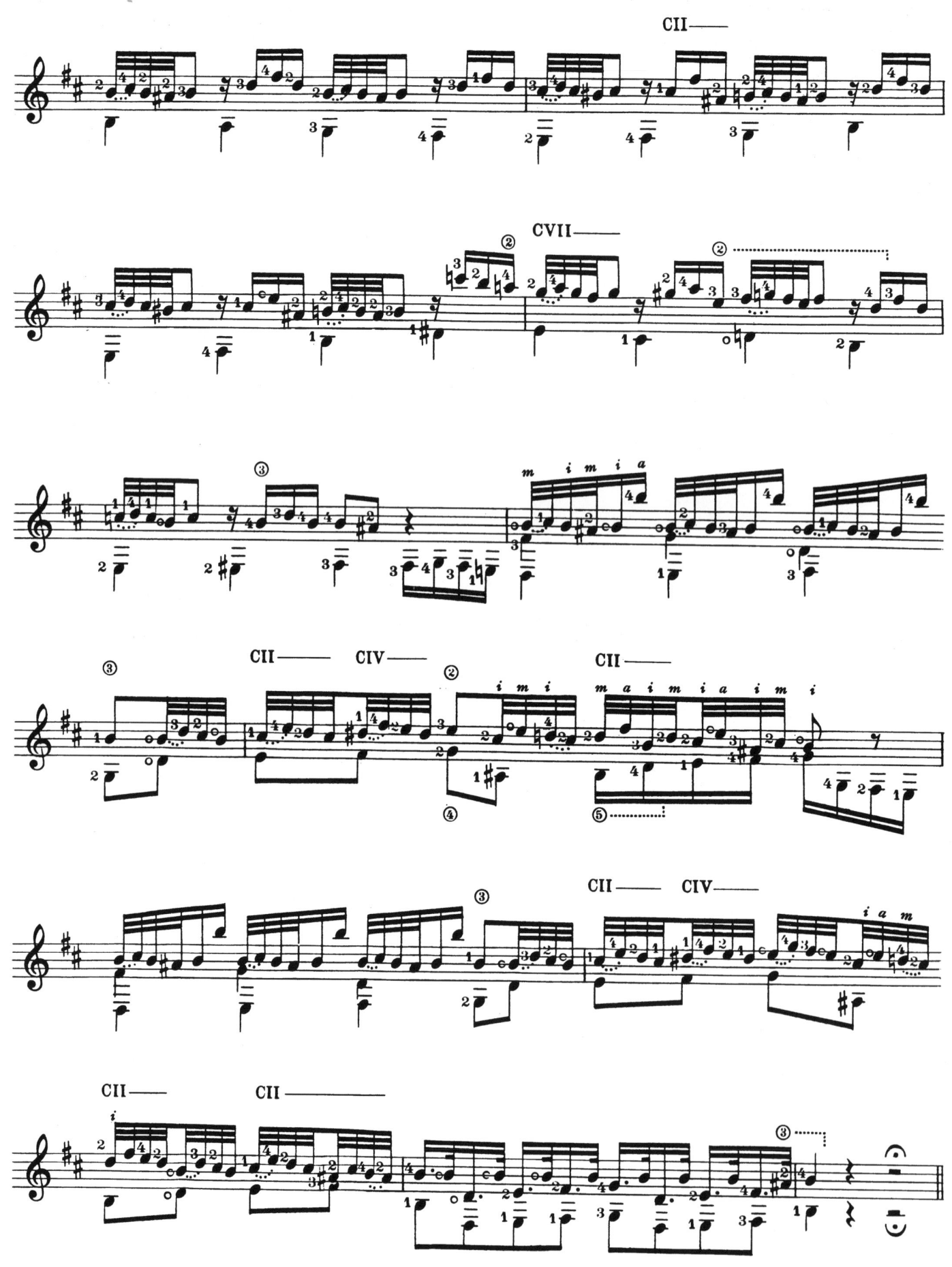